THE DOODLES OF SAM DIBBLE

by J. Press
illustrated by Michael Kline

Grosset & Dunlap
An Imprint of Penguin Group (USA) Inc.

GROSSET & DUNLAP
Published by the Penguin Group
Penguin Group (USA) Inc., 375 Hudson Street, New York, New York 10014, USA
Penguin Group (Canada), 90 Eglinton Avenue East, Suite 700, Toronto,
Ontario M4P 2Y3, Canada (a division of Pearson Penguin Canada Inc.)
Penguin Books Ltd, 80 Strand, London WC2R 0RL, England
Penguin Ireland, 25 St Stephen's Green, Dublin 2, Ireland (a division of Penguin Books Ltd)
Penguin Group (Australia), 707 Collins Street, Melbourne, Victoria 3008, Australia
(a division of Pearson Australia Group Pty Ltd)
Penguin Books India Pvt Ltd, 11 Community Centre, Panchsheel Park,
New Delhi—110 017, India
Penguin Group (NZ), 67 Apollo Drive, Rosedale, Auckland 0632, New Zealand
(a division of Pearson New Zealand Ltd)
Penguin Books, Rosebank Office Park, 181 Jan Smuts Avenue,
Parktown North 2193, South Africa
Penguin China, B7 Jaiming Center, 27 East Third Ring Road North,
Chaoyang District, Beijing 100020, China

Penguin Books Ltd, Registered Offices: 80 Strand, London WC2R 0RL, England

Text copyright © 2013 by Judy Press. Illustrations copyright © 2013 by
Michael Kline. All rights reserved. Published by Grosset & Dunlap, a division of Penguin
Young Readers Group, 345 Hudson Street, New York, New York 10014. GROSSET &
DUNLAP is a trademark of Penguin Group (USA) Inc. Printed in the U.S.A.

Library of Congress Cataloging-in-Publication Data is available.

ISBN 978-0-448-46107-6   10 9 8 7 6 5 4 3 2 1

THE DOODLES
OF SAM DIBBLE

For the girls: Anäelle, Samantha, Cate, Hudson, and Maggie—JP

For my wife and best friend Vickie—MK

Chapter One
An Underarm Fart Doodle

 My name is Sam Dibble. I can ride my bike 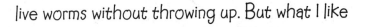 with no hands, make underarm farts, and eat

live worms without throwing up. But what I like

to do most is doodle.

My Logo

I think doodling is a lot of fun. It's like taking your pen for a walk and going someplace you've never been before.

I even like doodling at school.

I go to Colfax Elementary School.

My teacher's name is Mrs. Hennessey.

She teaches third

grade and has

superpowered eyes.

One eye looks

at the whiteboard,

and the other eye

sees kids fooling

around. Or doodling.

Which was exactly what I was doing in class

last week when I was supposed to be doing my

math work sheet.

As I was doodling, I realized that my birthday was in twenty-eight hours, seven minutes, and four seconds. Here's what I wished for:

1. A new bike because I messed up the old one.

2. New pens so I could draw more doodles.

3. The best birthday party ever. (Better than the space party with a rocket ride and moon bounce that Max Baxter, the biggest tattletale in third grade, had.)

Suddenly Max jumped up out of his seat.

"Mrs. Hennessey, Sam's doodling!" he

shouted.

"No, I'm not, Wax!" I shouted back. "I'm

writing something very important about my

birthday."

Everyone called Max "Wax," because one

time we had a contest to see who could pick

the most wax from our ears and he won.

Mrs. H. stared at me with her eye. "Sam, get back to work! And no doodling!"

My grandpa once said that everyone in our family doodles. Even Cousin Caveman Dibble doodled. But Grandpa says my cousin got in trouble because he wrote on the walls of his cave.

I picked up my pencil and tried to figure out the first math problem.

It was too hard, so I turned the work sheet over and drew my favorite doodle on the back.

Demo Dan is the world's greatest wrestler. Demo has a tattoo of two cars on his chest, and when he pumps up his muscles, the cars crash.

It was quiet in the room because everyone was doing their schoolwork. Except for me.

After lots of minutes, Mrs. H. said, "Time's up. I need someone to collect the math work sheets."

Wax's hand shot up in the air. "Mrs. H., please, please, pretty please let me do it!"

Mrs. H. gave Wax the nod. "And when you're done collecting, bring them up to my desk."

Wax marched up and down the aisles. Then he stopped at my desk. "Hand over your work sheet, Doodle Dork," he demanded.

I shook my head. "Wax, I can't give it to you because I didn't do any math."

"I don't care." Wax snorted. "Mrs. Hennessey said I have to collect them, so hand it over."

Wax tried to grab my work sheet, but I got to it first.

NOM NOM

2+2

84 12

9

"Ty an get it naw, Wax," I mumbled as drool

dripped down my chin.

"I'm telling," Wax declared. "And you're

going to be in big trouble."

Here was my birthday wish number four:

10

Chapter Two
A Dead Fish Doodle

Robert Chen sits next to me. He's

supersmart, and he's my best friend.

"Sam, did you really swallow your math

work sheet?" he asked.

"Nah, I spit it out, and Mrs. H. gave me

another one. She said I have to do it for

homework."

One time I didn't bring in my homework

because I couldn't finish copying it from

Robert.

Mrs. H. clapped her hands to get our attention. I think teachers learn clapping in Teacher School.

"Class, today we're going to discuss the person you admire the most. Who would like to start?"

Robert raised his hand. "My dad's my favorite person," he said. "He promised to take me fishing this summer. I admire him for that."

"I admire Mrs. Hennessey," Nicole McDonald said.

"Me too," said Meghan Diaz. "She's the best teacher in third grade."

Meghan and Nicole sit next to each other in the back of the room. They tell everyone they're twins, but they're not even sisters. Girls do dumb things like that.

Next Wax said he was picking his parakeet,

Tweety. "He's my best friend, and he can roll

over and play dead."

Duh, everyone knows a parakeet's not a

person. And even my goldfish, Charley, once

floated upside down and played dead.

Then *it* was my turn. "Mrs. Hennessey,

I'm picking Demolition Dan. He's the world's

greatest wrestler."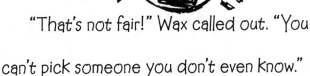

"That's not fair!" Wax called out. "You

can't pick someone you don't even know."

"I do know him. And he's coming to my

birthday party because I'm his number one fan."

 "Sam's lying," Wax said. "I saw him cross his

fingers and that means he's telling a lie."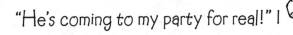

"He's coming to my party for real!" I

shouted back, stuffing my hands in my pockets

and crossing my fingers inside.

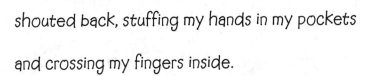 "That's enough," Mrs. H. warned. "It's okay

to admire someone you don't personally know—

for example, the president of our country or a

famous athlete."

I turned and smirked at Wax.

"Just remember," Mrs. H. continued, "your

written reports are due on Tuesday. Now it's

time for Reading Corner."

The Reading Corner has a bookcase full of

books. It's even got cushions on the floor so

we can lie down.

I was busy

looking for a book

that didn't have

a lot of pages

when Reginald

Cook walked over.

No one ever wants to get too close to

Cookie because he farts.

"Hi, Sam," Cookie said.

"I can't wait to meet

Demo Dan.

He's my favorite wrestler."

Before I had a chance

to say anything, Wax came over. "Let's call a truce, Dribble," he said. "Might as well since my dad's making me go to your dumb old birthday party."

My mom said I had to invite Wax since his dad is her new boyfriend.

I thought that stunk worse than Cookie's farts!

Chapter Three
A Barf Doodle

When we were done reading, Mrs. H.
told Wax and me to look up George
Washington on the computer.
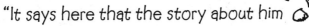 Presidents' Day was next week. All the
presidents have the same birthday, so kids get
a day off from school.
"It says here that the story about him
chopping down a cherry tree isn't true," Wax
declared, pointing to the screen.

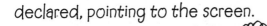

"Yeah, well, my grandpa says he saw George Washington do it."

"Dribble, my dad says your grandpa's always making stuff up. Just like you made up that Demo Dan's coming to your party."

"He is coming, Wax. Just you wait and see."

"Ha, Dribble! If Demo Dan comes to your party, I'll give you all my bobbleheads."

Wax has an awesome bobblehead collection. He's got lots of important people like Spider-Man, Snoopy, and the snowboard dude Shaun White. And he's even got a bobblehead of himself. He can keep that one.

"Okay," I told him.

Wax Bobble

CHEAP

"But if he doesn't show up," Wax said

with a sly grin on his face, "then I get all your

Halloween candy."

I could feel a knot in my stomach. It was like the time I ate the school lunch and barfed.

Halloween's my favorite holiday. One time I got a dollar bill because the guy said he forgot to buy candy. I'm saving it so I can get more ants for my ant farm before my mom sees they are missing.

I thought about the bet for a whole minute. "It's a deal, Wax."

Mrs. H. looked up from her desk. "No more talking. Sam and Max, get back to work."

"I'm working," Wax declared. "But Sam isn't."

"Yes, I am!" I yelled back.

I typed "Demolition Dan the world's greatest wrestler" into the computer. Then I pressed Enter.

Beep, beep, beep. The computer made a loud noise.

"Mrs. Hennessey, the computer's not working," I called out. "It must be busted."

"Sam, you should know certain websites are off-limits on school computers."

"But, Mrs. Hennessey, I have to find Demo Dan's e-mail address. It's really important."

"No e-mails, Sam!" Mrs. H. said. "You're supposed to be looking up George Washington, not contacting friends."

I went back to my desk and flipped through the pages of my assignment notebook.

"Whatcha doing, Sam?" Robert asked,

looking over my shoulder.

"I'm writing a letter to Demo Dan to invite

him to my party."

"I thought he was already coming!"

Robert said.

I felt a little bad about making the

promise before I knew for sure that he could

come. But, really, Wax had given me no choice!

"What if he's got a match that day or his

tour bus breaks down or he gets hurt and has

to go to the hospital?" Robert asked me.

I shook my head. "Demo Dan won't miss it

for anything because I'm his number one fan."

And if he does, I'll be in the biggest

trouble of my life!

#1

Chapter Four
A Water-Out-the-Nose Doodle

Dear Mr. Demo Dan, (You can call me Sam since we're almost best friends.) Today's your lucky day!!! You're invited to my birthday party tomorrow. We're having pizza for lunch, and my mom's baking chocolate chip cookies. If you come, all the kids in my class will say it was the best party ever, and I won't have to give Wax my Halloween candy.

Your number one fan,

Mr. Sam P. Dibble

The bell rang, and I quickly folded my letter and stuffed it in my backpack.

"Class, it's time to go to the library," Mrs. H. said. "So let's get a move on."

I raced to the front of the room and got in line behind Rachel Woolsey. She's the most popular girl in my class, and she hates me.

One time at lunch I made water come out of my nose, and Rachel said I was the grossest kid in third grade.

Rachel turned around to face me. "Hi, Sam," she said. "I'm having kids over at my house next week. Can you come?"

Wow, I'd never been to Rachel's house.

Robert told me she's got a swimming pool and

a basketball hoop in her backyard.

"Sure, I can. I just have to let my mom know

where I'm going."

"And, Sam, can I come to your birthday

party?"

"Yeah, you're invited. Do you like Demo

Dan? He's going to be there."

"Me and my brother watch all his matches

on TV. I love when he stands on the ropes and

jumps into the ring."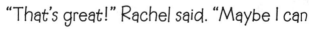

I put my hands behind my back and

crossed my fingers. "Demo Dan's bringing his

championship belt with

him, and he's letting

everyone wear it."

Rachel sucked in her

breath. "Wow, that's totally awesome."

"Yeah, I know. And he's giving everyone at

my party a signed autograph."

"That's great!" Rachel said. "Maybe I can

get an extra one for my brother."

"And guess what? Demo Dan said he's

getting me front-row seats to his next match."

I uncrossed my fingers because Grandpa

says if I cross them *too many times* they'll get

stuck together, and I won't be able to pick my

nose.

"What kind of birthday cake are you

having?" Rachel asked. "At my party I had a

princess cake with buttercream icing and spun-

sugar flowers."

"My grandpa is making my cake, and it's a

surprise."

"Your grandpa must be an awesome baker. I

can't wait to see your cake."

One time Grandpa told me he baked a

cake for a king in Egypt. But then the king

died so they had to bury him inside the cake.

Mrs. H. waved to Rachel and me. "Let's

get going," she said. "We don't want to be late

for library."

I smiled as I walked down the hall. I couldn't

wait for my birthday. Only twenty-six hours,

fifteen minutes, and nine

seconds to go!

Chapter Five
A Man-Eating Shark Doodle

My whole class marched into the library, and everyone scrambled to find a seat.

"Let's sit here," I told Robert, pointing to the last table at the back of the room.

"There are two seats at the table up front. Why are we sitting here?"

"I don't want Mrs. Booker to see me, that's why," I whispered.

Mrs. Booker is the school librarian. I bet

she got picked because her name sounds like

a book. Grandpa says our name is from the

Vikings, and it means "dodo" in Viking words.

"Okay, Sam, why don't you want her to see you?" Robert asked.

"Here's the deal. Remember the book I got out from the library a few weeks ago?"

"You mean the one about man-eating sharks? The pictures were awesome."

"Well, the book's lost, and I can't find it. Now I'll have to pay a really big fine, maybe even a million dollars." **$ $!**

"Wow, what if you don't have the money?"

"Mrs. Booker will make me read all the books in the library. Even the ones with no pictures."

Robert's eyebrows shot up. "Gee, that could take a really long time. Like, you won't finish until you're really old."

Mrs. Booker passed by our table, and I slid down a little lower in my chair.

"Good morning, class," she said. "Today you will be using the library's resources to learn more about the person you admire the most."

Meghan and Nicole were sitting next to us. They each had a red thingy in their hair.

Meghan raised her hand. "Mrs. Hennessey said I can't pick her, so I'm picking Helen Keller. She was blind and deaf and learned how to talk and read."

Then Nicole said, "I'm picking Martin Luther King Jr. He had a dream about civil rights for everyone."

"Those are great choices," Mrs. Booker told them. "Just be sure to make good use of the Internet, encyclopedias, and nonfiction books."

"What are you looking up?" Robert asked me.

"I'm finding out where Demo Dan lives.

Then I can mail the letter I wrote to him."

"How are you going to do that? The

library's computer is blocked just like the one in

class."

"I've got it all figured out. I'll get

Mrs. Booker to look it up on her special teacher

computer. Then she'll tell me what it says."

Everyone was running around the library

looking up stuff. Wax walked over and sat down

next to Robert and me.

"Hey, Dribble," he started. "You know that

book you got out from the library, the one

about man-eating sharks?"

WAX=
1200
CALORIES

"Yeah, what about it?"

"I need it because I'm looking up stuff about sharks, and I can't find it on the shelves."

"Sam lost it," Robert blurted out. "And now he has to pay a million-dollar fine."

Wax took one look at me. Then he whipped around and chased after Mrs. Booker.

"Sam lost a library book!" he shouted. "And he can't find it."

Maybe I could look for a book about magic tricks that'll teach me how to make Wax Baxter disappear!

Chapter Six
A Superhero Stamp Doodle

After library, Mrs. Booker said it was okay

for me to keep looking for the shark book and

she wouldn't make me read all the books in the

library if I never found it. YAY!

Next we had art. Here's why I like art class:

1. Miss Murphy is the art teacher, and she

   says it's okay to doodle because

   Leonardo da Vinci doodled and he's a

   famous artist.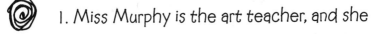

2. We never get any homework, so I don't have to make up stories about why I didn't do mine.

3. There are mobiles hanging from the ceiling, and if you blow on them, they move. Cookie said they'll move if you fart but I've never tried that.

"Good morning, class," Miss Murphy said. "Today you're going to make a collage. Each of you will cut out words and pictures from newspapers and magazines and glue them onto poster board. You can also use other found materials such as feathers, leaves, and scraps of paper."

Meghan, Robert, Nicole, and I sat at a long table next to the art supply closet. At home, I keep my special things in my closet. They're next to my dirty clothes so no one will touch them.

Meghan raised her hand. "Miss Murphy, can Nicole make my collage? She's a better artist than me."

Miss Murphy made one of those fake grown-up smiles. "Meghan, I'm sure you'll do a very good job. Now everyone come up and choose your materials."

I walked over to the art supply table. Miss Murphy put out some really weird things. There were bird feathers, magazine pictures, and stamps of really important people.

Grandpa says one time he found an airplane stamp, but he threw it away because something was wrong with the picture.

Wax was grabbing stuff for his collage.

"Dribble, my artwork will be in a museum one day, so don't copy it."

"I can do my own art, Wax, and it'll be better than yours."

Wax walked away, and I picked out my art

supplies. All I needed was a glue stick and one

stamp.

When I got back to my table, Meghan and

Nicole were working on their collages.

"We're giving our collages to Demo Dan,"

Meghan said. "It's a surprise."

Nicole started to giggle. "He's cute," she

added.

Yuck! Girls say silly things like that.

I watched Robert as he tried to glue a

feather onto his paper. "This stinks," he said.

"The feather keeps sticking to my fingers."

Now I had to get to work. I pulled out the

envelope Mrs. Booker had given me. She had

written Demo Dan's name and the address of

his fan club on the front.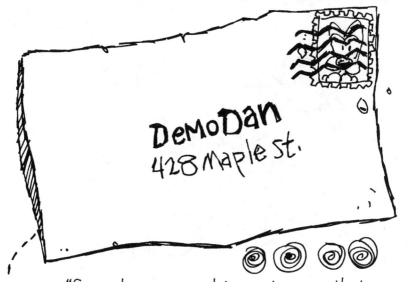

DeMoDan
428 Maple St.

"Sam, why are you gluing a stamp on that

envelope?" Robert asked. "You're supposed to

glue stuff on this big paper."

Sometimes Robert wasn't so smart. "Duh,

it's so I can mail my letter to Demo Dan."

MAIL HONK!!

"That stamp is old, and see the black lines? That means someone already used it and the mailman won't deliver your letter," Robert explained.

"Yeah, he will. Grandpa says when he delivered the mail he only threw away letters no one would want to get."

I grabbed a marker and on the back of

the envelope I wrote: VERY IMPORTANT

LETTER FOR DEMO DAN ABOUT MY

BIRTHDAY PARTY.

Then I put the envelope in my backpack.

Hopefully, I would remember to mail it!

Chapter Seven
A Vampire Doodle

Here's what's great about three o'clock:

School's over for the day.

I grabbed my jacket from my locker and

threw my backpack over my shoulders. Then

I raced down the steps two at a time and

headed out the door.

Robert was supposed to come to my

house after school, but he couldn't. He had to

get braces on his teeth.

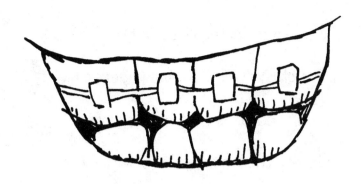

If I had crooked teeth, I wouldn't get

braces because then I couldn't chew gum. Also,

if I stuck my finger in an outlet, I'd light up like

a Christmas tree.

Cookie was waiting outside in the school yard. We always walked home together because his house is next door to mine.

"Do you think Demo Dan would autograph my poster of him?" Cookie asked me. "I can bring it when I come to your party."

"I don't know, but I guess he would."

Cookie pumped his fist. "Thanks a million,

Sam. You're the greatest, and your party will

be the best one ever!" SAM

There's a mailbox on the corner by my

house. I dropped my letter to Demo Dan in

the box and waved good-bye to Cookie.

When I got to my house, I stuck my head

inside the front door. "Hello, I'm home," I

yelled. "It's me, your favorite third grader."

Grandpa was on the couch in the living room watching TV. "Hi, Sammy-boy!" he shouted. "How'd your day go?"

I dropped my backpack in the hallway and plopped down next to him. "It was kind of good. I got all my spelling words right, but I got in trouble for doodling on my math work sheet."

Grandpa turned to look at me. "That's my boy!" he said, patting me on the back. "I'm real proud of you, Sammy-boy."

"But, Grandpa, aren't you mad I got in trouble?"

"Why should I be? We always get in

trouble. Why, one time . . ."

Before Grandpa could finish what he was

saying, my mom walked into the room. "Don't

forget we're meeting Jeff and his family for

dinner tonight."

When my mom talks about Wax's dad,

her eyelids flutter up and down. Maybe she's

sending a secret message to someone about

Jeff.

"Is Wax coming, too?" I asked, hoping she'd say he couldn't come because he got stuck somewhere.

QUICKSAND HA-HA!!

"Of course, Max will be there. You boys should learn to be friends. He's a very nice young man."

↖ false advertising

"But, Mom, you don't understand . . ."

 "Please, Sam, just try a little harder. It'll mean so much to Jeff and me."

 Here's the weird thing about Wax's dad: He owns a funeral home, and he hangs around dead people all day.

 When Mr. Baxter sees me, he always wants to slap five. But I know he just touched a dead person, so I tell him I just pooped in the toilet and didn't wash my hands.

I've never even seen a dead person except in a movie about vampires. But I closed my eyes so it doesn't count.

I really, really, really didn't want to go out to dinner with Wax, so it was time for me to get sick and I had to do it fast.

"Mom, I'm not feeling well," I moaned. "I can't go out because everyone will catch my sickness, and they'll have to close down the restaurant."

My mom put her hand on my forehead. "Sam, you're as cool as a cucumber. There's no reason you can't go."

It's bad enough I have to see Wax in school. But if my mom married his dad, we would be brothers, and that made me feel really sick!

Chapter Eight
An Albert
Einstein Doodle

The whole way to dinner, I was hoping Wax

and his dad wouldn't show up, but they were

standing outside the restaurant waiting for us.

"Hello, Grandpa," Wax said, shaking

Grandpa's hand. "I see you've brought along

Sam. Funny, I thought he'd be home redoing

his math work sheet." HA Ha

I was about to tell Wax he had monkey's

breath when I looked down and saw his little

sister, Lucy.

"Hi, Sam Doodle-Head," Lucy said,

whistling between her missing front teeth. "I'm

coming to your birthday party. My daddy said

I could."

"Lucy can't wait to meet Demo Dan," Wax

added. "She'll be very disappointed if he isn't

there."

No way was Lucy coming to my party. It's only for kids in my class and not dumb little sisters. **NO WAY**

"Mom, tell her she can't come . . . ," I pleaded.

My mom pulled me aside. "What's this about Demo Dan?" she asked. "Are you up to something that I don't know about?"

I cleared my throat and looked down at the floor. "I invited Demo Dan to my party, that's all. It's no big deal. And he hasn't said he'll be there, but I know he's coming."

My mom was still shaking her head when the hostess came over and took us to our table.

"The kids can sit together," Wax's dad

said.

Wax flashed me a cheesy smile and sat

down next to me. Then Lucy sat down on my

other side.

The waiter took our order and walked

away. Then I felt someone kicking me under the

table. "Quit it or else . . . ," I hissed in Lucy's ear.

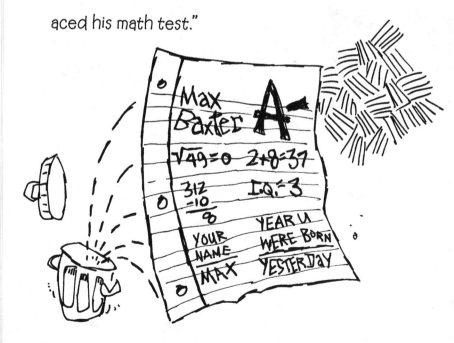

"Daddy, Sam's saying mean things to me,"

Lucy whined. "He's not being very nice."

Wax's dad tapped his water glass. "Quiet,

everyone. I have good news to share. Max

aced his math test."

Grandpa swallowed a mouthful of water and let out a loud burp.

"How nice, Max," my mom said. "You should be very proud."

"Max said he copied off a smart kid who sits next to him," Lucy blurted out. "And he gave her candy so she wouldn't tell."

One time I copied off some kid. I gave him my rubber band ball and five Gummi Bears, but he told, anyway.

Wax's face got all red. "That's not true! Lucy is always making stuff up."

"No, I'm not!" Lucy declared. "Max, you even said so."

"Lucy is also very bright," Wax's dad told my mom. "Her teacher said she could be another Albert Einstein."

Maybe she could be a dangerous criminal

and have her picture on a wanted poster.

"Did you say Al Einstein?" Grandpa said.

"We used to pal around together. He was

always coming up with crazy ideas."

"Honey, your dad should see a doctor,"

Wax's dad whispered to my mom. "I don't think

he's all there."

Grandpa cupped his hand around his ear.

"What's that you're saying, Baxter? You have

toenail hair?"

"Sam's grandpa is funny," Lucy declared.

Then she kicked me again really hard.

I jumped up from my chair and accidentally

knocked my water glass over.

"Dribble, you did this on purpose," Wax

cried, mopping water off his pants.

"It's all Lucy's fault!" I protested. "She's

the one who should get in trouble."

"Daddy, Sam hurt my feelings," Lucy
whined. "And now I'm not going to his birthday
party."

Ha! Maybe this was my lucky day after all!

Chapter Nine
A Goose Bumps Doodle

Finally, my birthday was in no hours, zero minutes, and nothing seconds.

My mom got me the bike I wanted.

Grandpa said he would've bought me something special but my mom wouldn't let him.

I got dressed and headed into the kitchen. Grandpa had a giant spoon in his hand, and he was mixing something in a big bowl.

"Happy birthday, Sammy-boy," Grandpa said. Then he put down his spoon. "Why the long face?"

"Today's my birthday, but I still haven't heard from Demo Dan. If he doesn't show up, I could be in really big trouble."

"Well, you never know if he's coming or he's not. One time I invited Blackbeard the Pirate to my birthday party."

"Wow! Did he show up?"

"Nope. Said he was too busy."

I spent the rest of the morning helping

put up the decorations for my party.

My mom got balloons and a hand-printed

banner that said Happy Birthday, Sam.

Just after lunch, the doorbell rang. Maybe

it was Demo Dan! I raced down the hall and

opened the front door wide.

It was Wax and his dad.

Wax stood back as his dad walked inside.

"Happy birthday, Dribble," Wax said. "I can't

stay long because I have a baseball game, and

my dad said that's more important than your

party."

Then I looked down and saw Lucy. "Happy

birthday, Sam Noodle-Doodle," she said. "My dad made me come to your party. Here's your present. Max got it for Christmas, but he didn't want it."

I grabbed the present from Lucy. The wrapping paper was torn, and it had pictures all over it of Santa Claus.

Wax's dad walked over and patted my shoulder. "When's the big guy showing up?" he asked, looking around.

"Yeah, Dribble, why isn't Demo Dan here yet?" Wax asked. "You said the party's starting at two, and he's already five minutes late."

I checked my Spider-Man watch. "Wax, don't you know anything? Famous people always come late."

The doorbell rang again. It was Cookie, Robert, Meghan, Nicole, and Rachel.

"Happy birthday, Sam," Cookie said. "Here's your present. My mom picked it out. It's an ugly sweater."

"I got you a book," Rachel said. "It's about a boy who's a wizard and makes people disappear."

Wow, how did Rachel know that was just what I wanted?

Next, Robert handed me a brand-new

basketball. "After your party, we can go shoot

some hoops," he said.

"Me and Nicole got you some new markers

so you can draw more doodles," Meghan said.

"When's Demo Dan getting here?" Nicole

asked.

"Uh, I think really soon."

Meghan scrunched up her face. "Are you

sure he's coming?"

"I swear on the

grave of my dead

fish, Charley, he'll be

here," I told her.

Nicole shivered. "I have goose bumps all over. This is going to be the best day of my whole entire life."

Robert took me aside after everyone went into the living room. "What's the deal with Demo Dan? Why isn't he here yet?"

"Hmm, maybe a lion escaped from the zoo and he had to capture it? Or maybe aliens kidnapped him and took him to their planet?"

Robert shook his head. "If Demo Dan doesn't show up, Wax gets all your Halloween candy. Then what're you going to do?"

Last year when I blew out the candles on my birthday cake, I made a wish:

This year I thought I would have to wish that Halloween was canceled!

Chapter Ten
Balloon Stomp Doodle

I looked at my watch again. It was two

thirty, and there was still no sign of Demo Dan.

Lucy was on the couch next to her dad.

"I'm bored," she said, yawning. "This party's no

fun. I want to go home."

"Be patient, Lucy," Wax's dad said. "Demo

Dan will be here any minute." ooTick Tock...

My mom pinched her lips together and

took a deep breath. It was like the time I told

her the bathroom flooded because I forgot to
turn off the water.

"Sam has a very vivid imagination," she said

to Wax's dad.

I was glad Mom was not turning me in.

"Now, let's play a game," my mom continued.

"I'll give out a great prize at the end."

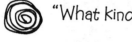 "What kind of prize?" Wax asked. "Did it

cost a lot of money?"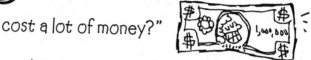

Wax's dad laughed. "Wax is a born leader.

One day he'll have a very important job."

"We're going to play balloon stomp," my mom said. "It's really lots of fun. First you tie a balloon around your ankle, then you run around trying to pop everyone else's balloon."

"The winner is the player whose balloon doesn't get popped," Robert added.

My mom brought out a bunch of balloons, and everyone tied one around their ankle. Then she put her hand up in the air.

"Ready, set, go!" she said, giving the signal for the game to start.

Wax shuffled over to Lucy and stepped on her balloon. "Daddy, Wax broke my balloon," Lucy cried. "Now I can't win the prize."

Next, Wax went after my balloon. He grabbed hold of my arm so I couldn't get away.

"That's cheating!" I shouted. "The rules say you can't hold on to a player."

"You're just a sore loser, Dribble," Wax snarled as he lifted up his foot and stomped down hard on my balloon. "So what? I popped your balloon fair and square."

Wax's dad stepped up and said, "Max, that's

enough! Either play fair or we're going home."

Finally! Two points for Mr. Baxter!

Wax slinked over to the couch and sat

down.

"Everyone's a winner," my mom announced,

passing out candy bars.

"I'm allergic to chocolate," Wax said,

handing his candy bar back to my mom. "I want

a different prize."

"Max," Mr. Baxter said, shooting him a

look. He really didn't like the way Wax spoke to my mom.

Before Wax could say anything else, the doorbell rang. "Maybe it's Demo Dan!" Robert shouted.

"It's about time," said Wax. "I thought he'd never show up."

Meghan and Nicole hugged each other and started dancing around the room. Girls did weird things like that.

"Yippee," said Cookie. "I can't believe I'm meeting Demo Dan in person."

I ran down the hall. Demo Dan was finally here!

Chapter Eleven
A Giant Sinkhole Doodle

I opened the front door wide and saw Grandpa! He was standing there with a bowl on his head and a towel knotted around his shoulders.

Wax stuck out his jaw. "Wait a minute," he said. "You're not Demo Dan. You're just Sam's grandpa."

"Think again, Max Baxter," Grandpa said, flexing his muscles. "You're looking at The Grampinator, a WFG champion. That stands for 'World Famous Grandpa,' in case you can't figure it out."

"But where's Demo Dan?" Meghan asked. "He was supposed to sign my poster."

"Yeah, mine too," said Cookie.

Grandpa pumped up his chest. "Me and Demo met in the ring last night, and I won the match. It was a piece of cake."

"How'd you do it?" Robert asked. "No one's ever beaten Demo Dan."

"I got him with my secret weapon," Grandpa said. "It's the 'Grandpa Hug.' Those bums can't take all that loving. They cry like a baby and give up."

I stared at the floor hoping something would swallow me up.

Suddenly, the fire alarm in my house

screeched a loud *BLEEP, BLEEP, BLEEP!*

I sniffed the air. "Something's burning!

Look, there's smoke coming from the kitchen!"

"Quick, everyone out of the house!" my

mom yelled. "I'll call the fire department."

Cookie was right behind me. "This is

awesome," he said. "It's the best party I've ever

been to."

Wax's dad grabbed hold of Lucy's hand.

"Don't be afraid," he reassured her. "We have

an excellent fire department in our town."

Wax caught up to me as we ran down my

front steps. "Tough luck, Dribble. Looks like

your birthday presents are going up in smoke."

"Wax, are you going home?"

"Nah, I'm sticking around. The party stinks,

but it's going to get better when I win our bet."

We all rushed outside and heard the roar

of a fire engine.

The fire truck stopped in front of my

house. A firefighter wearing an oxygen mask

jumped down from the cab.

"Step aside!" he shouted. "I'm going in."

After a few minutes, he came back out.

"All's clear," the firefighter told my mom. "No damage done, except for the cake you had in the oven."

Grandpa clapped his hand to his head. "Oh no!" he cried. "I forgot about Sam's birthday cake."

"The important thing is no one was hurt," my mom said with her arm around me. "We can always get another cake."

The firefighter took off his mask. "Hello, I'm Firefighter Dan. I'm guessing today's your special day. I'd like to wish you a happy birthday."

"Sam, thank Firefighter Dan," my mom said.

I opened my mouth to talk, but nothing came out. Then I blinked my eyes a few times. I couldn't believe who was standing right in front of me!

Chapter Twelve
A Nose
Booger Doodle

Everyone crowded around Demo Dan.

Their mouths were hanging open. Even Wax

didn't say anything.

OPEN 4 Business

Grandpa had a big smile on his face. "Well, I'll be. About time you showed up. I could only cover for you for so long. Kids nowadays are smart as whips. I didn't fool 'em, but you can't say I didn't try."

"Can you stay for my party?" I asked Demo Dan. "There's no birthday cake, but my mom baked chocolate chip cookies."

"I'd love to stay, but I'm on duty today. It's my job to keep our town safe," he told me.

Meghan put her hands on her hips. "How can you be a firefighter if you're a wrestler?"

Demo Dan laughed. "That's a good question. Many wrestlers have other jobs."

"What kinds of jobs?" Cookie asked.

"Well, some wrestlers deliver the mail and some work in construction. Others are police officers and teachers."

"Are they moms and dads, and do they

have kids like us?" Nicole asked.

"We sure are. I have a wife and two little

boys."

Robert raised his hand like he was in

school. "Mr. Demo, where do you train

for your matches?"

"Since I live right here in town, I train at our

local gym. But now I have to get going, kids.

It's time for me to get back to work."

Everyone let out a loud, "Boo!"

"But I'd like to invite all of you to my next

match," Demo Dan added. "And it'll be my

treat."

Then everyone shouted, "Hooray for Demo Dan! He's the world's greatest wrestler!"

Demo Dan hopped up into the fire truck and waved good-bye.

The fire truck rumbled loudly as it headed back down my street. That's when I saw Wax standing off by himself. He was busy doing something.

I walked over to talk to him. "Guess I won our bet, Wax," I said. "But we can still be friends."

"Who cares?" Wax said, shrugging his shoulders. "You can have my bobbleheads because my dad said he's buying me new ones, anyway."

"Thanks, Wax. And you can keep the one that looks like you."

"Let's make another bet, Dribble," Wax said slyly. "I bet you can't stop doodling for a whole week."

"Okay. And I'll bet you can't stop telling on everyone."

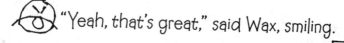 "Yeah, that's great," said Wax, smiling.

"Let's shake, and it's a deal."

Wax put out his hand, and I reached out to

take it. We shook, and I felt something slimy.

I flipped my hand over and took a look.

Gross, it was Wax's booger!

Chapter Thirteen
A Whoopee Cushion Doodle

My party was over, and it was back to school on Tuesday. Now my next birthday was in three hundred sixty-two days, fifteen minutes, and four seconds.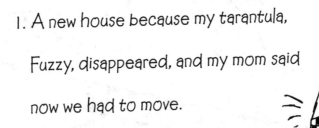

Here's what I wanted:

1. A new house because my tarantula, Fuzzy, disappeared, and my mom said now we had to move.

2. A rocket-building kit so I could send

Wax Baxter to the moon.

3. A new whoopee cushion because

Mrs. H. took away my old one.

Mrs. H. was in the back of the classroom helping Cookie with his math. Everyone was working on math except me. I had to write my report on the person I admired the most.

I didn't write it when I was supposed to. It was my birthday, and there should be a rule that says kids don't have to do homework on the weekend when it's their birthday parties.

OFFICIAL
NO
HOMEWORK
ON BiRthday
party weekends

Yay!

I grabbed a piece of paper and started

writing:

THE PERSON I ADMIRE THE MOST

The person I admire the most is two people.

The number two person is Demo Dan. He's the

world's greatest wrestler, and when he has a

match he climbs up on the ropes and jumps down

on top of the other wrestler, but then he goes

home and puts out fires and keeps people safe.

The number one person for me, though, is my

grandpa. He used to be a kid,

but then he got old. Now he's really old, like, maybe a hundred years old. I like the stories Grandpa tells because they're really funny. And when I get in trouble for doodling, Grandpa says it's not such a bad thing 'cause he got in trouble all the time. But the best thing about Grandpa is he is my family, and he's my best friend.

THE END

After I gave my report, Wax said it wasn't fair that I picked two people when everyone else had to pick one.

Mrs. H. said it was okay and told Wax to sit down.

Robert said he really liked my report, and maybe I'd do better on my report card this time.

Cookie said it was the best report ever, and he wanted to go over to Demo Dan's house and play video games.

Meghan and Nicole said my report made them cry. Girls do dumb things like that.

Now I'm working on a new doodle. But that's another story.

SNEAK PEEK OF

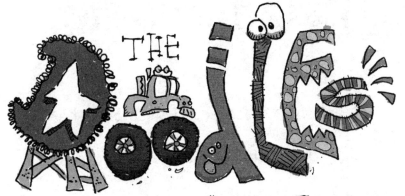

THE DOODLES

OF SAM DIBBLE

Double Trouble

A Gross Pizza Doodle

After Mrs. H. collected our letters, she told us some exciting news! We were going to elect a class president!

"Today is Tuesday," she said. "On Friday we'll vote. The class president should be someone who sets an example of good behavior and is helpful to others. He or she also should be someone who you think will be a responsible leader."

Everyone started talking about how cool it would be to be class president.

"Settle down," Mrs. H. said. "Being class president is a serious job. The class president will help me make some of the class rules. Also, the president will help me pick some of the other students for jobs, like messenger or pet monitor or cleanup monitor," she continued.

Rachel Woolsey raised her hand. "Mrs. Hennessey, I'd like to run for president."

Rachel's the most popular girl in my class, and she hates me. One time at lunch I slurped spaghetti through my teeth, and she said I was the grossest kid in third grade.

"Thank you, Rachel," Mrs. H. said.

My best friend, Robert Chen, sits next to me. He's really smart and lets me copy off him.

"Sam, if Rachel is president she'll make a rule that the boys have to do girly things," he whispered.

Eeek! I don't want to do that!

Next, Wax raised his hand. "I want to be president," he declared. "And when I get elected we'll have pizza for lunch every day."

Then Wax shot a look at me. "And I know just who I'll make cleanup monitor!"

"We need one other candidate," Mrs. H. continued, looking around the room.

I looked over at Wax. He was making a list in his notebook. It was probably a list of all the horrible things he'd make me do.

Maybe I should run.

Here's why I wanted to be class president:

1. I could boss Wax around.
2. Everyone would think I'm super cool.
3. Maybe I'd get to meet the real president !!!

I raised my hand.

About the Author

J. Press has taught millions of kids how to doodle. She majored in doodling at Syracuse University and went on to get a master of doodling at the University of Pittsburgh. At home she enjoys spending time doodling with her children and grandchildren. In her spare time she . . . guess what? You're right! She DOODLES!

About the Illustrator

Michael Kline (Mikey) received a doctorate in applied graphite transference from Fizzywiggle Polytechnic and went on to deface (sorry, *illustrate*) over forty books for children, the most notable being one with J. Press involving an ambulance-chasing peanut. The deadly handsome artist calls Wichita, Kansas, home, where he lives with his very understanding wife, Vickie, felines Baxter and Felix, and two sons.